The Wobbuffet Village

POKéMON junior

#15

Adapted by S. E. Heller

SCHOLASTIC INC.
New York Toronto London Auckland Sydney
Mexico City New Delhi Hong Kong Buenos Aires

ISBN 0-439-35805-1

Designed by Carisa Swenson

12 11 10 9 8 7   4 5 5/0

Printed in the U.S.A.

First Scholastic printing, May 2002

CHAPTER ONE

A Wobbuffet Festival

Pikachu, a yellow mouse Pokémon, was resting. It was on the shoulder of Ash, its trainer. But Ash did not get to rest. He was walking with his friends Misty and Brock.

"Whew. Guess we have to keep walking, huh?" said Brock.

"Yeah," said Ash and Misty. They were tired.

Misty noticed a guidebook in front of them on the path. She picked it up.

"*Pika?*" Pikachu wondered who the book belonged to.

Just then, a funny blue Pokémon popped up behind them.

"Wobbuffet!" cried Ash.

Pikachu wondered if this Wobbuffet belonged to Jessie and James. The two teenagers belonged to a group called Team

Rocket. They always followed Ash and his friends around. They wanted to steal Pikachu for their boss, Giovanni.

"If Wobbuffet is here, then Team Rocket might be close by," warned Brock.

The friends looked around for Jessie and James. They were surprised to see more Wobbuffet instead.

"*Wobbuffet! Wobbuffet!*" cheered the group of Wobbuffet. They led Pikachu and its friends into a village. There were Wobbuffet everywhere.

"This is Wobbuffet Village," a boy told them. "Every person has their very own Wobbuffet."

"Why Wobbuffet?" asked Misty.

"It is a joy to be with a Wobbuffet," said the boy, smiling.

"We just love them."

Misty pointed to the boy's T-shirt. It had a blue Pokémon painted on the front. "You even wear Wobbuffet clothes?" asked Misty.

The boy laughed. "Only during the Wobbuffet Festival," he told them. "Once a year we have a party to celebrate our Pokémon. The village is being decorated right now."

"*Pika pika!*" Pikachu was excited to hear about a festival.

The boy gave the friends a tour of the village. There were

5

Wobbuffet decorations everywhere. The villagers and their
Wobbuffet all looked so happy.

"*Brrr!*" Togepi, Misty's tiny
Pokémon, bounced in her arms. It
wanted to stay for the party. So
did Pikachu.

CHAPTER TWO

Wobbuffet Welcome

Meanwhile, Team Rocket had also found the Wobbuffet Village. Jessie, James, and their talking Pokémon, Meowth, fell to their knees.

"We have not eaten in three days," moaned Meowth. They were all hungry.

"*Wobbuffet!*" Jessie's Wobbuffet came out of its Poké Ball.

"Hey, who told you to come out of your Poké Ball?" Jessie demanded.

Wobbuffet didn't pay Jessie any mind. Because suddenly, there were Wobbuffet all around!

"Oooo!" A lady named Lulu hurried toward Team Rocket. "You have a Wobbuffet, too!" she cried. "I am so glad that you brought your Pokémon to our village."

Team Rocket did not know why
anyone would be happy to see a
Wobbuffet. They were still mad
that Wobbuffet had been forced
on them after they lost a
Pokémon battle.

But Lulu did not know that Team Rocket was always up to no good. Anyone with a Wobbuffet was welcome in Wobbuffet Village. So she invited them to her house. She gave them a feast of hamburgers. She even gave

Jessie's Wobbuffet a special ribbon to wear. Jessie, James, and Meowth laughed. They thought the yellow ribbon looked funny, but Wobbuffet liked it.

When they were finished eating, Lulu showed Team Rocket a giant statue of Wobbuffet.

"This is our festival symbol," Lulu told them.

"It's huge!" cried Meowth.

"Why would you bother to celebrate Wobbuffet?" Jessie muttered.

"What did you say, dear?" Lulu asked.

"Oh, nothing. Just how great that big Wobbuffet is," said Jessie.

"*Wobbuffet!*" cried Wobbuffet. It liked the big statue. And the people in the village were pleased to see a guest Wobbuffet. It was not long before Team Rocket was invited to another feast.

CHAPTER THREE

Under Attack

On a nearby cliff, three bullies looked down into Wobbuffet Village.

"The villagers are getting ready for their party," said the first boy. He had red, spiky hair. "It is the perfect time for revenge."

The bully took a Poké Ball out

of his pocket. He called for his Pokémon, Hitmonlee, to come out.

"Come out, Machoke!" cried another bully.

"Come out, Primeape!" said the third.

The three Pokémon were strong and tough. They were ready for a Pokémon battle.

Meanwhile, Pikachu and its friends were having fun playing with the Wobbuffet in the park. They were surprised when a little boy came running up to them.

"Someone attacked Annie's Wobbuffet!" the little boy cried.

Pikachu and its friends ran to help. Wobbuffet's trainer, Annie, was crying. Her Wobbuffet lay on the ground, badly beaten.

"What happened?" asked Misty.

"Out of the blue, they attacked my Wobbuffet," Annie said.

"That is terrible!" cried Ash.

"Who would do such a thing?" asked Brock.

"This boy's Wobbuffet was attacked, too!" a man called from a hill above.

"There were three of them," the boy told them. "They attacked my Wobbuffet for no reason."

"Three of them?" asked Ash. There were three members of Team Rocket. And whenever there was trouble, Team Rocket was usually behind it.

CHAPTER FOUR

Team of Thieves

At that moment, Team Rocket was peeking into a building. Festival food was piled high. It looked good.

"Let's take it all," said Meowth, licking its lips.

Jessie and James agreed. But they could not steal the food right

away. Someone was coming! Team
Rocket hid their faces behind
some leaves.

It was Pikachu and its friends.
They were running. Another
Wobbuffet had been attacked.

As they ran past, Ash saw
Team Rocket trying to hide.
Pikachu was not surprised to see
its enemies.

"What do you think you're
doing?" demanded Misty.

"All right, we admit it. We did
it," said Jessie.

"I knew they were the team of three attacking everybody's Wobbuffet!" said Ash angrily.

"Whoa, hold on. We have not done anything yet," said James.

"We were just getting a bite to eat," said Meowth.

Just then, Lulu appeared. She did not believe that Team Rocket

was to blame. "Do you have any proof?" she asked Ash.

"Well . . . no," said Ash.

"They have a Wobbuffet. They must be good people," said Lulu. She even invited Team Rocket to stay at her house.

Still, Pikachu and its friends were not so sure. But just then, a girl ran to tell them about another Wobbuffet attack.

So it was true, thought Pikachu. *Team Rocket could not be in two places at once.*

"We are not responsible for every bad thing that happens," said Jessie.

"Fine, then," said Ash.

Pikachu and its friends headed into the village.

"Good luck finding the criminals," James called after them.

"Quick, let's take the food before someone else comes," said Jessie.

CHAPTER FIVE

Revenge

When Pikachu and its friends arrived at the park, the bullies and their fighting Pokémon were there. They had just beaten another Wobbuffet.

"*Pikachu!*" Pikachu was angry.

"Do you know who they are?" Ash asked a boy next to him.

"Yes," said the boy. "They came here a while ago. They set their fighting Pokémon against everyone instead of training them themselves. But Lulu's Wobbuffet beat them in a Pokémon battle."

Now the three bullies wanted revenge. "Today we have

come to pay you back!" cried the leader.

"We will defeat every Wobbuffet in this village," declared another bully.

"Oh, no!" cried the boy. He ran to get Lulu and Officer Jenny.

Team Rocket was filling their sack full of food when they saw the boy, Lulu, and Officer Jenny running through the streets of Wobbuffet Village.

"Hurry!" the boy cried.

"What's happening?" asked Meowth.

CHAPTER SIX

No Battles Allowed

"I am ready to face you in a Pokémon battle," said Ash.

"You will be the perfect warm-up for our next Wobbuffet battle," said the leader of the bullies.

"Chikorita, I choose you," Ash called. A small, green Grass Pokémon appeared. Misty called

Poliwhirl, a Water Pokémon with a swirl on its round body. Brock called Golbat, a Flying Pokémon that looked like a bat. They were all ready for battle.

"Hitmonlee. Rolling Kick!" called the bully leader.

Ash told Chikorita to use Vine Whip.

Just then, the boy returned with Lulu and Officer Jenny.

"Stop everything!" said Officer Jenny. "Pokémon Battles are not allowed during the Wobbuffet festival."

Ash, Misty, and Brock looked at
Officer Jenny in surprise.

"*Pika?*" asked Pikachu. *Why?*

Officer Jenny explained that
Wobbuffet was a peaceful
Pokémon. It never made the first
attack in a battle. So, to honor its
peaceful spirit, the villagers

agreed not to have any Pokémon battles during the festival.

"So that is why the Wobbuffet did not fight back when attacked," said Brock.

Ash and his friends agreed to put their Pokémon away.

"You stop, too," Officer Jenny told the bullies. But they were not ready to leave.

"If you will not face us in a Pokémon battle, then we will break your Wobbuffet statue to pieces instead," said the leader.

CHAPTER SEVEN

Team Rocket to the Rescue?

Hitmonlee kicked the giant statue. Machoke and Primape pounded and punched.

"Stop!" cried Brock.

Behind some bushes, Team Rocket watched. Jessie's Wobbuffet was sad. Even Meowth felt bad for the kind villagers.

"*Wobbuffet!*" cried Wobbuffet.

We have to help!

As Team Rocket made plans,
Pikachu's cheeks sparked in anger.
The statue was covered with holes.
The crowd watched helplessly.

Just then Team Rocket floated
down in their hot-air balloon.

"Prepare for trouble," Jessie
warned the bullies.

"Make it double," cried James.

The fighting Pokémon and their
trainers were surprised to see
Team Rocket. They called

Hitmonlee, Machoke, and Primeape to battle Team Rocket's Pokémon.

"But Pokémon Battles are not allowed," Officer Jenny said.

"Breaking rules is what we do best," said Jessie, grinning. "Go Arbok!" she cried.

"Go Victreebel!" called James.

The Poison Grass Pokémon opened its wide mouth. It tried to eat Meowth.

"No!" James yelled. There was no time for mistakes.

"Hitmonlee! Rolling Kick!" the leader of the bullies called out the first attack.

Hitmonlee jumped and kicked with its powerful legs. Arbok fell backward.

"Arbok, Tackle," Jessie ordered.

Arbok dove at Hitmonlee headfirst. It stopped Hitmonlee's Rolling Kick Attack.

"Machoke! Karate Chop!" called the next bully. Machoke was strong. It struck Victreebel. The Grass Pokémon was hurt.

"Razor Leaf!" James called to Victreebel. The Plant Pokémon whipped sharp leaves. But Primeape knocked the leaves away with quick punches.

Now Arbok tried to use Wrap Attack.

"Hitmonlee. Hi Jump Kick!" called the leader.

Hitmonlee struck before Arbok had a chance to attack.

Hitmonlee's kick forced the Snake Pokémon to the ground.

"Machoke! Seismic Toss," called another bully. This was one of Machoke's strongest attacks. It picked Victreebel up and swung it in circles. It was beat.

"We cannot lose to weak Pokémon like yours," the leader of the bullies said, making fun of Team Rocket.

But Jessie would not give up the battle yet.

34

CHAPTER EIGHT

Wobbuffet Wins Again

"We still have our Wobbuffet,"
Jessie told the bullies. "Show
them what you can do, Wobbuffet!"

"*Wobbuffet!*" Jessie's Wobbuffet
was happy to join the battle.

"Go Hitmonlee! Use Jump
Kick!" called the bully leader.

As Hitmonlee raced at the blue

Pokémon, Jessie told Wobbuffet to use Counter Attack. Wobbuffet shut its eyes. Its yellow ribbon started to glow. Soon Hitmonlee's kick struck Wobbuffet. But the Pokémon had formed a glowing shield. The fighting Pokémon was thrown backward.

Machoke tried Karate Chop next. Wobbuffet's Counter Attack blew it away. Primeape tried Fury Swipes. It was no match for Wobbuffet. Primeape spun through the air like a ball.

"Wow!" said Ash.

"*Pika!*" Pikachu was amazed.

"My Wobbuffet really is strong," said Jessie.

"Attack all at once," the bully leader told the fighting Pokémon.

Jessie told Wobbuffet to keep up the Counter Attacks. Wobbuffet was ready.

Hitmonlee used Hi Jump Kick.
Primeape used Fury Swipes.
Machoke used Karate Chop.
When they struck, Wobbuffet's
Counter Attack was stronger than
ever. The fighting Pokémon were
blasted through the sky!

"It looks like this battle is over,"
Lulu told the bullies. "Now *get
out* of our village!"

The bullies were not so brave
without their Pokémon. They ran
away as fast as they could.

CHAPTER NINE

Food Fight

Finally, the festival statue was safe. The whole village cheered for Wobbuffet.

"*Wobbuffet!*" Wobbuffet smiled. *I was happy to do it!*

"Still, rules are rules," said Officer Jenny.

Jessie and James understood.

"I wish the best to all you Wobbuffet," said Jessie as Team Rocket lifted off in their hot-air balloon.

"*Wobbuffet!*" All the Wobbuffet in the village thanked Team Rocket.

"Team Rocket sure was different today," said Brock.

Pikachu watched the balloon float away. The little yellow Pokémon could not believe that Team Rocket had been so nice. Then suddenly, the balloon

stopped. A metal hand reached
down to pick up a large sack.

"That is the village food
supply!" cried Officer Jenny.

"I guess they did not change
after all," said Ash. He and
Pikachu and their friends ran
after the thieves.

"Go Staryu!" cried Misty. A star-

shaped Water Pokémon came out of its Poke Ball. "Staryu, Tackle!"

Staryu turned circles through the air. It tore through Team Rocket's balloon. Down they fell.

Team Rocket could not get away now. But they still tried to fight for the food. Jessie called Arbok. James called Weezing.

"Since you cannot use your Pokémon to battle . . ." said Jessie.

"We will win!" James laughed.

But Officer Jenny shook her head. "We are outside of the

village. Anyone can have a
Pokémon Battle here."

Now Jessie and James were
worried.

"*Wobbuffet!*" Even Jessie's
Wobbuffet was worried.

Pikachu squeezed its cheeks.
Electricity started to spark.

"Pikachu, Thunderbolt!" cried Ash.

As Pikachu's powerful attack
hit the balloon, Team Rocket shot
through the air.

"Looks like Team Rocket's
blasting off again!" cried Jessie,
James, and Meowth.

CHAPTER TEN

A Happy Village

Soon the villagers had fixed the Wobbuffet statue. Pikachu and Togepi had fun dancing with their friends.

"Brrr!" Togepi loved the festival.

"Pika!" Pikachu did, too.

Everyone was happy, and the

Wobbuffet statue glowed as
fireworks lit up the night.

Far away, Team Rocket sat
around their own fire. Jessie,
James, and Meowth felt sorry for
themselves. Only Jessie's
Wobbuffet stood up proudly.

"Wobbuffet!" Jessie's Pokémon was glad that it had helped to save the festival symbol. Happily, it thought about its Wobbuffet friends and the fun they were having in their happy village.